W9-AFA-808

DANCE ON A SEALSKIN

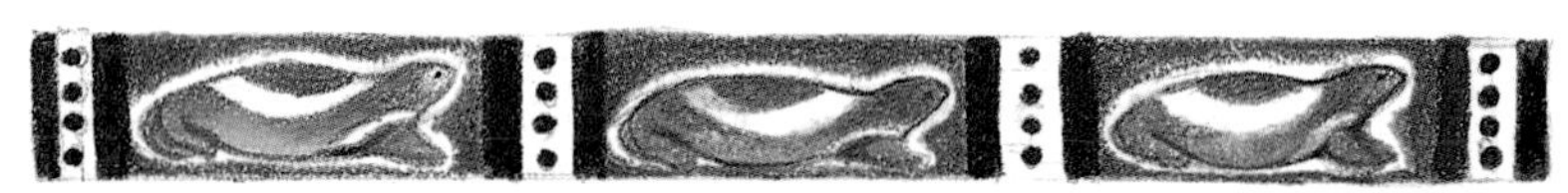

STORY BY BARBARA WINSLOW

ILLUSTRATIONS BY TERI SLOAT

ALASKA NORTHWEST BOOKS™

ANCHORAGE ♦ SEATTLE ♦ PORTLAND

Dedication

To our dear friends in Emmonak and Kotlik, at the mouth of the Yukon River, who taught us to dance, and much more

B. W. & T. S.

Acknowledgments

This story is based on the experiences of the author and illustrator while living and teaching in Yupik villages along the Yukon River and the Bering Sea in Alaska in the 1970s. Potlatch traditions vary from village to village. Traditions mentioned in this story are a blend of those we witnessed.
The author wishes to extend special thanks to Waska Charles from Emmonak, who read this manuscript, corrected the Yupik spellings for her, and urged her to get it published. And to Martina Redfox, also from Emmonak, who supported her in this endeavor.

Library of Congress Cataloging-in-Publication Data:
Winslow, Barbara, 1947–
Dance on a sealskin / by Barbara Winslow ; illustrations by Teri Sloat.
p. cm.
Summary: In honor of her grandmother, who passed away, Annie does her first dance at potlatch in her Yupik Eskimo village. Based on a Yupik Eskimo tradition.
ISBN 0-88240-443-1
[1. Yupik Eskimos—Social life and customs—Fiction. 2. Eskimos—Social life and customs—Fiction.] I. Sloat, Teri, ill. II. Title.
PZ7.W72995Dan 1995
[Fic]—dc20
94-40438
CIP
AC

Editor: Ellen Harkins Wheat
Designer: Elizabeth Watson

Alaska Northwest Books™
An imprint of Graphic Arts Center Publishing Company
Editorial office: 2208 NW Market Street, Suite 300, Seattle, WA 98107
Catalog and order dept.: P.O. Box 10306, Portland, OR 97210 Telephone: 800-452-3032

Printed on acid-free paper in Korea

Note to the Readers

This story is based on the Yupik Eskimo tradition of the "first dance," which can be performed at any age but is usually done before adolescence and can represent the person's officially becoming a community member. The dance is done in the *kashim* at a village potlatch—a social gathering for dancing, gift-giving, being with friends, and honoring the dead. The songs and dances performed at a potlatch can be ancient or new. Often they hold a powerful spiritual significance and are a means of conveying oral history.

The thundering beat of the walrus-skin drum lured Annie and her mother through the wintry night. Annie held her mother's hand tightly, taking courage from its warmth. Together with many other villagers, they were walking toward the round sod *kashim*. Everyone was laughing and talking, so no one noticed Annie's silence. Tonight was Annie's big night. Tonight she would do her first dance at potlatch.

Annie's hands trembled in the soft rabbit-skin mittens that Grandmother had made for her. Nervously she smoothed her colorful *qaspeq* over her fur *parkie* and looked down at her new *mukluks*. How Annie wished Grandmother could see her now.

She thought back to all the nights they had sat on the rough board floor of the kashim, watching the dancers bounce and sway to the beat of the drums. Grandmother had smiled proudly when Annie asked to dance too. They stood together to learn the dance that would be Annie's first dance. One was young and straight, the other old and bent, their eyes just alike.

But Grandmother was old, and one sad night, when the northern lights reached down to touch the rim of the earth, Grandmother went to be with her ancestors. Now Annie would dance alone.

Mother's gentle tug on Annie's sleeve brought her back to the present. The kashim loomed in front of them and soon they were at the door. Stooping, they entered the steamy interior.

In the light of the kerosene lamps, Mother and Annie could see many friends and visitors seated around the dark walls, laughing and talking.

Boom, boom, boom, pounded the drums.

"Ai-yii, ai-yii, ai-yii," chanted the men from their benches.

Annie's heart raced with the beat of the drums.

Mother and Annie sat near Aunt Olinka and Baby Olga. Annie nuzzled Olga's soft, rosy cheek and smelled her sweet warmth. She grinned when the baby tugged at her long black braids. Olga, like many of the village babies born recently, had been named after her Grandmother. The villagers believed that Grandmother's spirit lived on in a child of the same name.

Now Annie whispered in Olga's tiny ears. "Little Grandmother, I hope you will smile at me when I dance. That will help me to be brave."

The drumming filled the night, as dance after dance was performed in the center of the kashim. When Old Ivan knelt with the other men in his group to begin his dance, Annie watched closely. The women took their places around the kneeling dancers and smiled, knowing Ivan would make them laugh. The dance began.

Shaking their dance fans, Ivan's group acted out the old story of a bear hunt. One minute Ivan was chasing the bear,

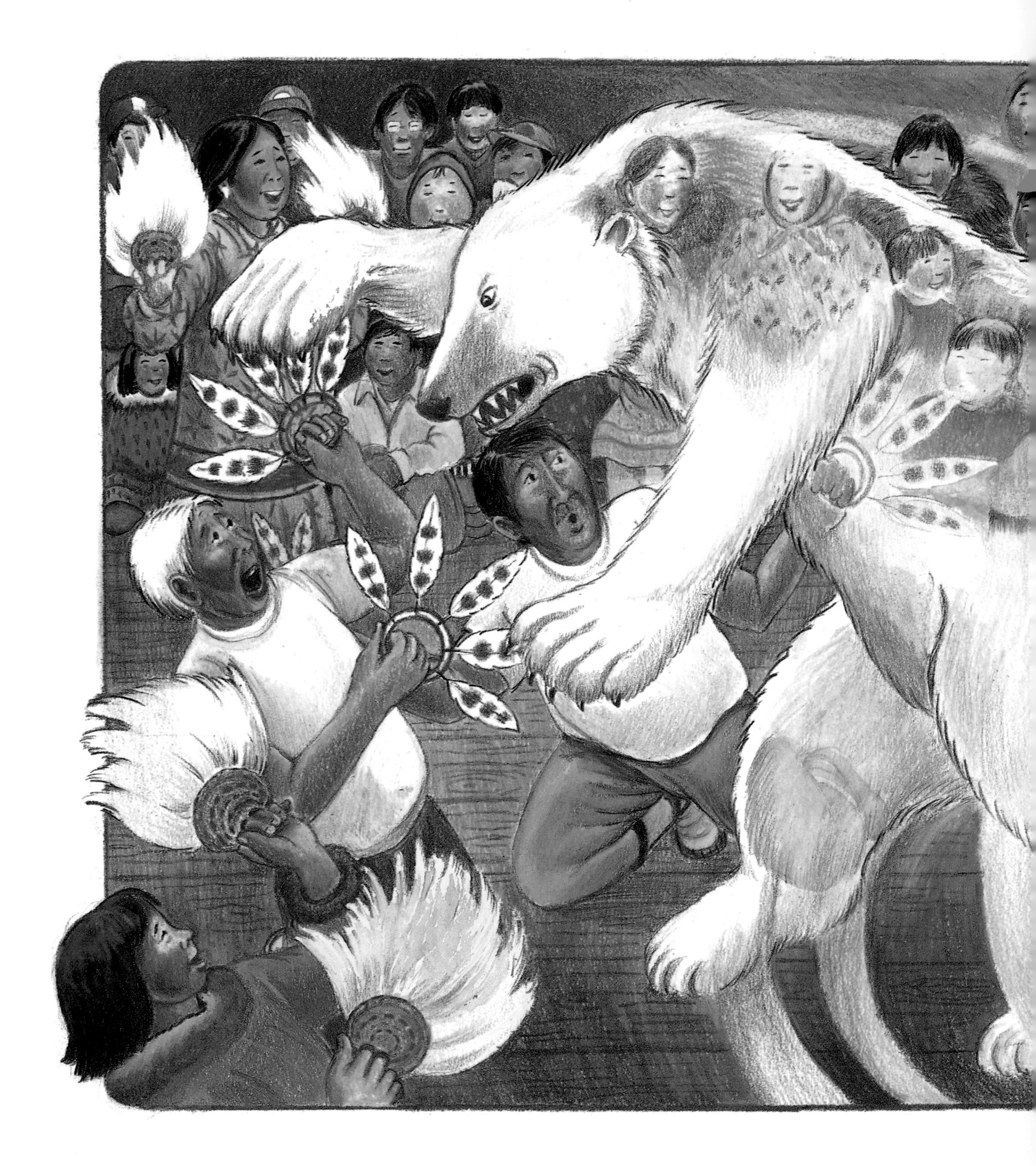

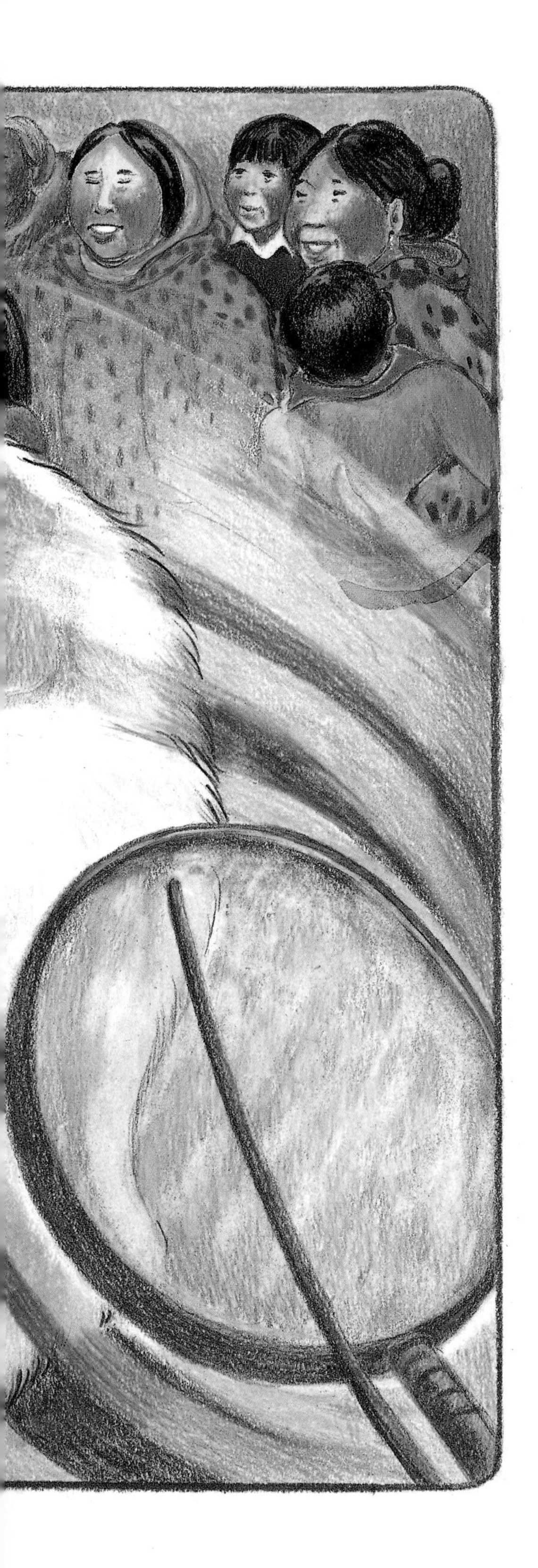

the next minute Ivan was running away. Faster and harder he bounced.

"More, more," shouted the people.

The drums raced on and Ivan fell to the floor, worn out.

Laughter and applause filled the kashim like thunder. Annie wondered whether everyone would like her dance too.

Another group began to dance the story of building a walrus-skin boat. Again, Annie watched closely. She could almost see the boat floating on the sea when the dance ended.

Boom, boom, boom. The drums beat out song after song.

"Ai-yii, ai-yii, ai-yii," chanted the men.

Annie watched the dancers, waiting for her song to begin. Each time the drums started to pound again, her heart skipped a beat. At last, she recognized the rhythm of her dance.

BOOM!
BOOM!

Mother pulled Annie to her feet and tied a crown of fur snugly around her forehead. Next she fitted a wolverine belt around Annie's waist.

Then Mother gave Annie her new dance fans. The long graceful strands of reindeer hair were tipped with snowy owl feathers and quivered with a life of their own. The wood handles were carved in the shape of ptarmigans, just as Grandmother's had been. Annie's hands shook as she reached for the fans, and Mother gave her a quick squeeze for courage.

They made their way to the center of the room where Annie's father waited for them, holding a smooth sealskin. It was silver, just like Grandmother's silver hair. He spread it on the floor for Annie to dance on. This was an honor that she would never have again.

Annie stepped forward and stood in the center of the sealskin. Her parents took their places with the other members of Annie's group. Then the drums began to sound. Keeping her eyes firmly on the dancer kneeling in front of her, Annie began to dance.

Though her knees shook, Annie bounced up and down to the beat. She and the other dancers moved together to tell the story of a daring walrus hunt on the sea ice.

At first the dancers moved slowly and gracefully, mimicking a hunter stalking a walrus. The dancers swayed, their hands and bodies moving to imitate careful steps across dangerous ice.

Suddenly the walrus spotted the hunter and wriggled to escape. Faster and faster moved the dancers. Wilder and faster beat the drums. Faster and faster ran the hunter.

Boom, boom, boom.

"Ai-yii, ai-yii, ai-yii."

"Pamyua, pamyua, pamyua," shouted the crowd. *"More, more, more!"*

Swiftly ran the hunter. The walrus neared the edge of the ice and open water.

Boom, boom, boom.

M!
OM!

Annie's eyes sparkled and her braids bounced against her shoulders. Her fans swayed gracefully before her. The shaking of her knees became one with the rhythmic beating of the drums and the chanting of the men.

Hurry, Hunter, hurry, pounded the drums.

The walrus slipped into the sea and the hunter was left alone.

"Pamyua, pamyua, pamyua," shouted the crowd.

And then, on one last frenzied beat, it ended!

The room exploded in laughter and applause, and the tired dancers moved off the floor. Grandmother's laugh reached Annie's ears. Baby Olga was smiling in Aunt Olinka's arms.

Annie stood alone on the silver sealskin. The drums began a soft and muffled beat. She kept her eyes lowered respectfully and extended her dance fans before her. Annie's father spoke. "In honor of our grandmother who died this winter, and to show pleasure in our daughter on the night of her first dance, we wish to give gifts to you, our friends."

EANUT
ROBERTSO

Annie's parents gathered the gifts. First they touched the gifts to Annie's hands to show they were from her, then her parents began to pass them out. There were mittens and gloves for the elders, aprons and dishtowels for the women. Father offered ax handles and fish traps to the men. The children all received candy and gum. Everyone was given a helping of *akutaq,* Eskimo ice cream.

It was a night of pleasure, and Annie's heart was warm and full. But she had one last gift to give.

Stepping off the silver sealskin, Annie picked it up and carried it to Baby Olga. As she kissed the round pink cheeks of the baby girl, Annie spread the sealskin on the floor beside her.

"This is for you, Little Grandmother. For your first dance."